THE SEATTLE PUBLIC LI

The Sun, the Moon, and the Stars

Poems collected, written, and illustrated by
Nancy Elizabeth Wallace

Houghton Mifflin Company Boston 2003

Acknowledgments

Warm thanks to my editor, Amy Flynn, art designer Maryellen Hanley, my agent, George Nicholson, the librarians in the reference department and the children's department at the Blackstone Library, and my writing group friends. All of these wonderful people have supported, guided, and nurtured me while I created this book.

Every effort has been made to trace the ownership of all copyrighted material and to obtain the necessary permissions to include these poems. In the event of any question arising as to the use of any material, the collector, editor, and publisher, while expressing regret for any inadvertent error, will be happy to make the necessary corrections in future printings.

Grateful acknowledgment is made for permission to print the following poems:

"Pillow Song" by Russell Hoban. Copyright © 1996 by Russell Hoban. Reprinted by permission of David Higham Associates Limited.

"Maytime Magic" by Mabel Watts. Reprinted with the kind permission of her sons, Stanley McEtchin and Robert McEtchin.

"The Sun" by John Drinkwater, from *All About Me* by John Drinkwater. Copyright © 1928 by John Drinkwater. Reprinted by permission of Houghton Mifflin Company. All rights reserved.

"The Summer Sun" by Wes Magee, from *Dragon Smoke* by Wes Magee. Copyright © 1985 by Wes Magee. Reprinted by permission of Wes Magee.

"Sunflakes" by Frank Asch, from *Country Pie* by Frank Asch. Copyright © 1979 by Frank Asch. Used by permission of HarperCollins Publishers.

"Day-Time Moon" by Dorothy Aldis, from *All Together* by Dorothy Aldis. Copyright ©1925–1928,1934,1939,1952, renewed 1953, © 1954–1956, 1962 by Dorothy Aldis, © 1967 by Roy E. Porter, renewed. Used by permission of G. P. Putnam's Sons, an imprint of Penguin Putnam Books for Young Readers, a division of Penguin Putnam Inc.

"Running Moon" by Elizabeth Coatsworth, from *The Sparrow Bush* by Elizabeth Coatsworth. Copyright © 1966 by Grosset and Dunlap, Inc., renewed. Used by permission of Grosset & Dunlap, an imprint of Penguin Putnam Books for Young Readers, a division of Penguin Putnam Inc.

"The Moon's the North Wind's Cooky" by Vachel Lindsay, from *The Collected Poems of Vachel Lindsay*, revised edition, by Vachel Lindsay. Copyright © 1925 by Vachel Lindsay. Reprinted with the permission of Simon & Schuster, Inc.

"Walking" by Lilian Moore, from *I Feel the Same Way* by Lilian Moore. Copyright © 1967 by Lilian Moore. Copyright © renewed 1995 by Lilian Moore Reavin. Used by permission of Marian Reiner for the author.

"If to the moon" and "Dragonflies" from *An Introduction to Haiku* by Harold G. Henderson. Copyright © 1958 by Harold G. Henderson. Used by permission of Doubleday, a division of Random House, Inc.

"Moon at the Beach" by Patricia Hubbell. Copyright © 2003 by Patricia Hubbell. Used by permission of Marian Reiner for the author.

"Crescent Moon" by Elizabeth Madox Roberts, from *Under the Tree* by Elizabeth Madox Roberts. Copyright © 1922 by B. W. Huebsch, Inc., renewed 1950 by Ivor S. Roberts. Copyright 1930 by Viking Penguin, renewed © 1958 by Ivor S. Roberts and Viking Penguin. Used by permission of Viking Penguin, an imprint of Penguin Putnam Books for Young Readers, a division of Penguin Putnam Inc.

"Moon Vine" by Harry Behn, from *Windy Morning* by Harry Behn. Copyright © 1953 by Harry Behn. Copyright © renewed 1981 by Alice Behn Goebel, Pamela Behn Adam, Prescott Behn, and Peter Behn. Used by permission of Marian Reiner for the author.

"Full Moon" by Walter de la Mare, from *The Complete Poems of Walter de la Mare*. Copyright © 1969. Reprinted by permission of the Literary Trustees of Walter de la Mare and the Society of Authors as their representative.

"Sleeping Outdoors" by Marchette Chute, from *Rhymes About Us* by Marchette Chute. Copyright © 1974 by E. P. Dutton. Reprinted by permission of Elizabeth Hauser.

"Until We Built a Cabin" by Aileen Fisher, from *That's Why* by Aileen Fisher. Copyright © 1946, 1974 Aileen Fisher. Used by permission of Marian Reiner for the author.

"Moon-Come-Out" by Eleanor Farjeon. Copyright © 1933, 1961 by Eleanor Farjeon. Reprinted by permission of Harold Ober Associates Incorporated.

www.houghtonmifflinbooks.com

The text of this book is set in Martin Gothic Medium. The illustrations are cut-paper collage.

Library of Congress Cataloging-in-Publication Data
The sun, the moon, and the stars / poems collected, written, and illustrated by Nancy Elizabeth Wallace.
p. cm.
Summary: A collection of more than thirty poems, some by the compiler, others by Walter de la Mare, Russell Hoban, Frank Asch, Jane Taylor, and others.
ISBN 0-618-26353-5
1. Sun—Juvenile poetry. 2. Moon—Juvenile poetry. 3. Stars—Juvenile poetry. 4. Children's poetry, American. [1. Sun—Poetry. 2. Moon—Poetry. 3. Stars—Poetry. 4. American poetry.] I. Wallace, Nancy Elizabeth.
PS595.S87S86 2003   811'.60809282—dc21   2002151186

Printed in Singapore TWP 10 9 8 7 6 5 4 3 2 1

dear friends are
        the sun, the moon, and the stars . . .
for Shaunee and Phil, Claudia and Duke, Cyd and Bobbi,
Robin and Bob, Sally and Rob, and always for Peter.
        with love,
                N.E.W.

Pillow Song

Moony, moony, silver deep
Ocean rock me to my sleep
Morning sunshine in my cup
Sing a song to wake me up.

—Russell Hoban

The Sun

I told the sun that I was glad
    I'm sure I don't know why;
Somehow the pleasant way he had
    Of shining in the sky,
Just put a notion in my head
    That wouldn't it be fun
If, walking on the hill, I said
    "I'm happy" to the sun.

—John Drinkwater

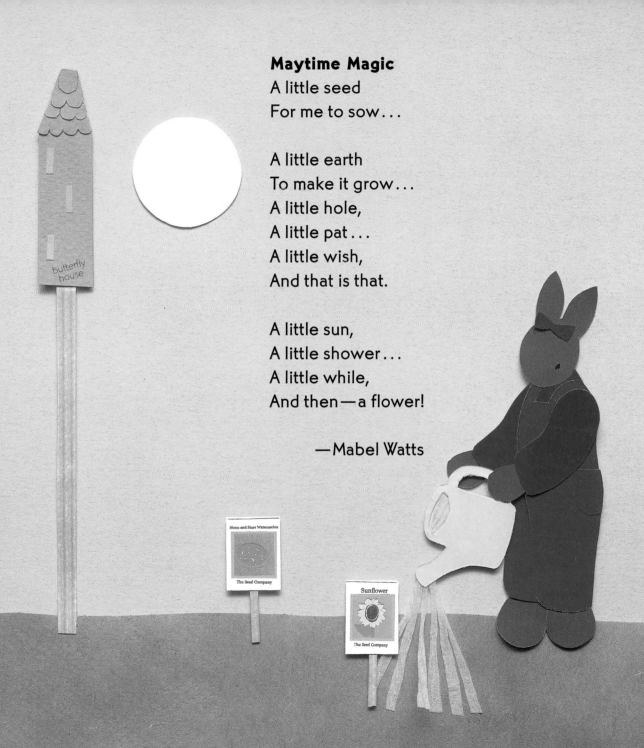

Maytime Magic

A little seed
For me to sow...

A little earth
To make it grow...
A little hole,
A little pat...
A little wish,
And that is that.

A little sun,
A little shower...
A little while,
And then—a flower!

—Mabel Watts

The Sun

There's sun on the clover
   And sun on the log,
Sun on the fish pond
   And sun on the frog,

Sun on the honeybee,
   Sun on the crows,
Sun on the wash line
   To dry the clean clothes.

—Louise Fabrice Handcock

The Summer Sun

Yes,
The sun shines bright
In the summer,
And the breeze is soft
As a sigh.

Yes,
The days are long
In the summer,
And the sun is king
Of the sky.

—Wes Magee

Sunflakes

If sunlight fell like snowflakes,
gleaming yellow and so bright,
we could build a sunman,
we could have a sunball fight,
we could watch the sunflakes
drifting in the sky.
We could go sleighing
in the middle of July
through sundrifts and sunbanks,
we could ride a sunmobile,
and we could touch sunflakes—
I wonder how they'd feel.

—Frank Asch

Sun

Sun,
  circle of warmth,
  circle of light,
    you are
      a star.

—Nancy Elizabeth Wallace

SUNdog*

SUNdog won't bite.
SUNdog won't bark.
But SUNdog wags her colors
in the sky, in an arc.

—Nancy Elizabeth Wallace

*A sundog is a small or incomplete rainbow.

Sunflower
Sunflower,
your face follows sunlight
east to west.

Sunflower,
does your head droop down at night
to rest,

unless
there's a full moon?

—Nancy Elizabeth Wallace

DAYS of the WEEK
SUNday
MOONday
TREEday
WATERday
CLOUDday
FROGday
STARday
If you could,
what would
YOU name them?

—Nancy
Elizabeth
Wallace

Sundae Sunday

The third Sunday in July is
National Ice Cream Day

				1	2	3
4	5	6	7	8	9	10
11	12	13	14	15	16	17
18	19	20	21	22	23	24
25	26	27	28	29	30	31

Day-Time Moon
In the morning when the sun
Is shining down on everyone
How strange to see a daytime moon
Floating like a pale balloon
Over house and barn and tree
Without one star for company.

—Dorothy Aldis

Running Moon
Sometimes when we drive out at night
I see the half moon, thin and white.
It runs beside us like a hound,
It's there whenever I turn round.

I say, "Good moon, come on, good moon!
It won't be long, we'll be home soon,"
And when we stop, there in the sky
The moon stands still, as still as I.

—Elizabeth Coatsworth

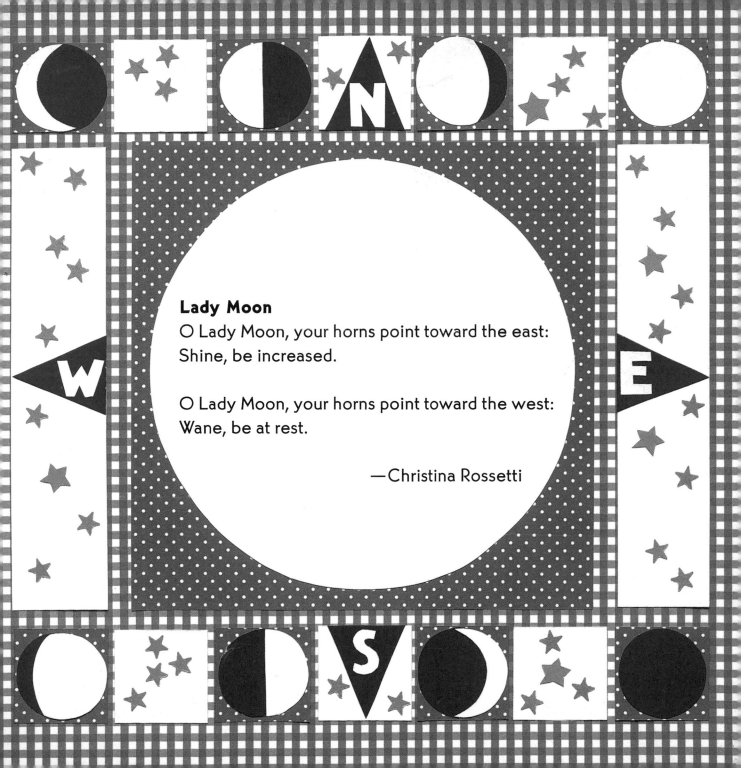

Lady Moon

O Lady Moon, your horns point toward the east:
Shine, be increased.

O Lady Moon, your horns point toward the west:
Wane, be at rest.

—Christina Rossetti

The Moon's the North Wind's Cooky
  (What the Little Girl Said)
The Moon's the North Wind's cooky.
He bites it, day by day,
Until there's but a rim of scraps
That crumble all away.

The South Wind is a baker.
He kneads clouds in his den,
And bakes a crisp new moon that . . . greedy
North . . . Wind . . . eats . . . again!

—Vachel Lindsay

Walking
I stop—
    it stops too.
It goes when I do.

Over my shoulder I can see
The moon is taking a walk with me.

—Lilian Moore

If to the moon
   One puts a handle—what
      a splendid fan

                    —Sokam

Dragonflies:
   All their frenzies quiet down—
      The young moon in the skies!

                    —Kikaku

I See the Moon
I see the moon,
And the moon sees me;
As we go sailing over the sea.
I sail water, she sails sky;
We are sailors, the moon and I.

—Traditional

Moon at the Beach
Moon,
your reflection
is a tambourine,
shaking in the waves.
Every fish is dancing!

—Patricia Hubbell

High Tide, Low Tide
High tide, low tide,
for eternity,
Moon plays tug-of-war
with the sea.

—Nancy Elizabeth Wallace

Crescent Moon
And Dick said, "Look what I have found!"
And when we saw we danced around,
And made our feet just tip the ground.

We skipped our toes and sang, "Oh-lo.
Oh-who, oh-who, oh what do you know!
Oh-who, oh-hi, oh-loo, kee-lo!"

We clapped our hands and sang, "Oh-ee!"
It made us jump and laugh to see
The little new moon above the tree.

—Elizabeth Madox Roberts

Moon Vine
One winter night
An old moon planted
Three enchanted
Seeds, gold bright,

One in frost
One under a tree
And one in a sea
Where it was lost.

And the frost became
A drop of dew,
And the tree grew
Comfortably tame

But soon soon
Like a silver weed
The lost seed
Blossomed a moon!

—Harry Behn

No Need to Light a Night Light
You've no need to light a night light
On a light night like tonight,
For a night light's light's a slight light,
And tonight's a night that's light.

When a night's light, like tonight's light,
It is really not quite right
To light night lights with their slight lights
On a light night like tonight.

—Anonymous

Full Moon

One night as Dick lay fast asleep,
   Into his drowsy eyes
A great still light began to creep
   From out the silent skies.
It was the lovely moon's, for when
   He raised his dreamy head,

Her surge of silver filled the pane
   And streamed across his bed.
So, for awhile, each gazed at each—
   Dick and the solemn moon—
Till, climbing slowly on her way,
   She vanished, and was gone.

—Walter de la Mare

Star-light, star-bright
First star I've seen tonight;
I wish I may, I wish I might
Have the wish I wish tonight.

—Traditional

Sleeping Outdoors
Under the dark is a star,
Under the star is a tree,
Under the tree is a blanket,
And under the blanket is me.

—Marchette Chute

Until We Built a Cabin

When we lived in a city
(three flights up and down)
I never dreamed how many stars
could show above a town.

When we moved to a village
where lighted streets were few,
I thought I could see ALL the stars,
but, oh, I never knew—

Until we built a cabin
where hills are high and far,
I never knew how many
    many
      stars there really are!

               —Aileen Fisher

Far-away-stars
Far-away-stars
Blink at me.
Wink at me,
and I'll wink back.

—Nancy Elizabeth Wallace

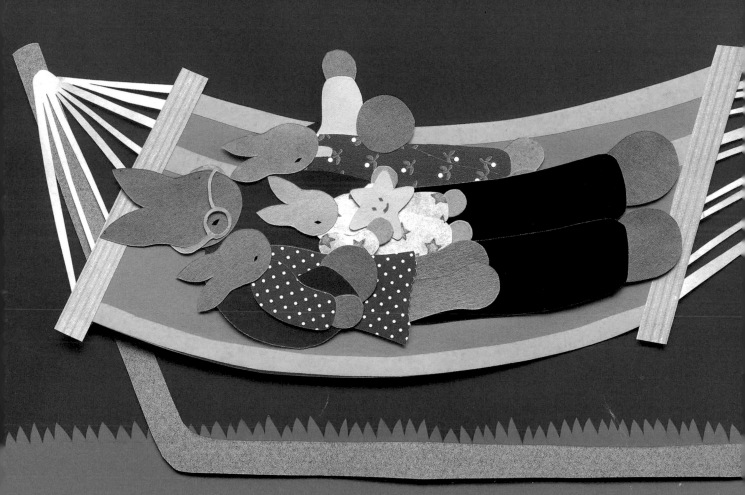

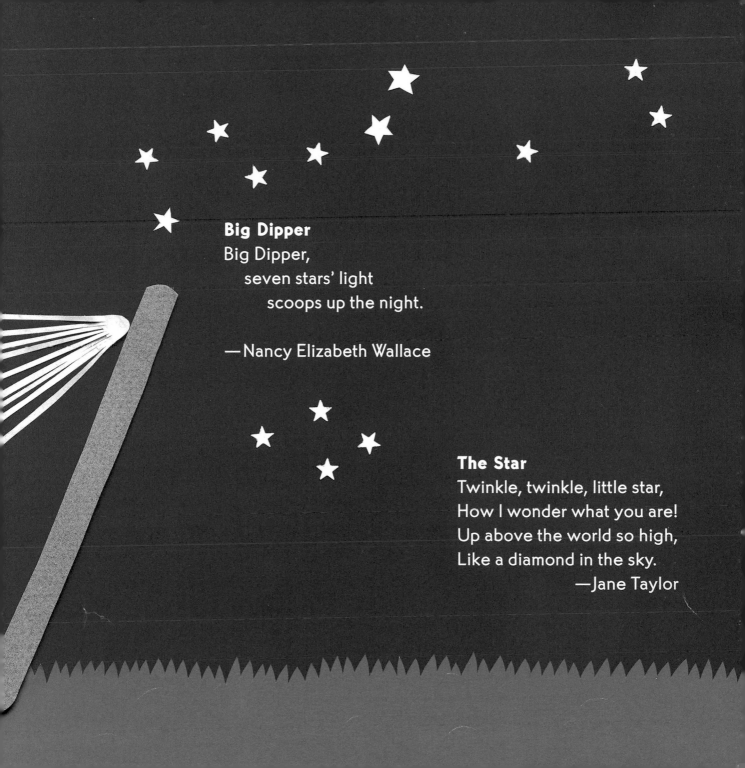

Big Dipper
Big Dipper,
   seven stars' light
      scoops up the night.

—Nancy Elizabeth Wallace

The Star
Twinkle, twinkle, little star,
How I wonder what you are!
Up above the world so high,
Like a diamond in the sky.
       —Jane Taylor

In the nighttime sky
A shooting star goes by
The world is a wondrous place

—Unknown

Last Song
To the Sun
Who has shone
  All day,
To the Moon
Who has gone
  Away,
To the milk-white,
Silk-white,
Lily-white Star
A fond goodnight
Wherever you are.

—James Guthrie

Moon-Come-Out

Moon-Come-Out
And Sun-Go-In,
Here's a soft blanket
To cuddle your chin.

Moon-Go-In
And Sun-Come-Out
Throw off the blanket
And bustle about.

—Eleanor Farjeon